For The
Best
Person in
The
World

THIS BOOK
WAS
WRITTEN BY

....

....

....

YOU ARE GOOD AT

....

....

....

YOU ARE SUPER AWESOME BECAUSE

. . . .

. . . .

. . . .

I WANT KNOW THAT
YOU ARE

....

....

....

I LOVE HOW YOU

. . . .

. . . .

. . . .

OUR FAVORITE THING TO DO TOGETHER IN SUMMER IS

. . . .

. . . .

. . . .

YOU ALWAYS HELP ME TO

....

....

....

I LIKE WHEN YOU CALL ME

....

....

....

I LOVE WHEN YOU COOK

. . . .

. . . .

. . . .

YOU LAUGH A LOT WHEN I

. . . .

. . . .

. . . .

YOU ARE SMARTER
THAN

. . . .

. . . .

. . . .

YOU WORK HARD AT

....

....

....

I LOVE WHEN YOU

. . . .

. . . .

. . . .

MY FAVORITE THING ABOUT YOU IS

....

....

....

IF I HAVE MILLION BUCKS
I WOULD BUY YOU

....

....

....

BEST THING ABOUT YOUR JOB IS

....

....

....

OUR FAVORITE THING TO DO TOGETHER IS

. . . .

. . . .

. . . .

I WOULD BUY YOU
A MILLION

....

....

....

YOUR FAVORITE FOOD IS

· ·

· ·

· ·

YOU LOVE WHEN I

....

....

....

MOVIE/TV SHOW THAT WE BOTH LOVE IS

. . . .

. . . .

. . . .

OUR FAVORITE THING TO DO TOGETHER IN WINTER IS

....

....

....

YOU ARE STRONGER
THAN

. . . .

. . . .

. . . .

YOU LOVE ME BECAUSE

....

....

....

I HAVE NEVER SEEN YOU

. . . .

. . . .

. . . .

YOU ARE SPECIAL
TO ME BECAUSE

. . . .

. . . .

. . . .

YOU MAKE EVERYONE

. . . .

. . . .

. . . .

YOU WILL ALWAYS BE MY

. . . .

. . . .

. . . .

YOU TAUGHT ME
HOW TO

....

....

....

I LOVE WHEN YOU TELL STORIES ABOUT

. . . .

. . . .

. . . .

YOU INSPIRE ME TO DO

....

....

....

I ENJOYED A LOT
WHEN WE WENT TO

....

....

....

I LOVE WHEN WE PRANK

....

....

....

I LOVE YOU A LOT
BECAUSE YOU NEVER

....

....

....

FUNNIEST THING YOU DO IS

....

....

....

OUR FAVORITE THING TO DO TOGETHER IN SPRING IS

....

....

....

I WAS AMAZED WHEN
YOU FIXED MY

. . . .

. . . .

. . . .

I FEEL SAFE WHEN YOU

．．．．．．．．．．．．．．．．．．

．．．．．．．．．．．．．．．．．．

．．．．．．．．．．．．．．．．．．

YOU DON'T CARE ABOUT

. . . .

. . . .

. . . .

I'M PROUD TO SAY YOU ARE

. . . .

. . . .

. . . .

YOU LIKE TO

....

....

....

OUR FAVORITE THING TO DO TOGETHER IN AUTUMN IS

....

....

....

I LOVED WHEN YOU SURPRISED ME WITH

. . . .

. . . .

. . . .

YOU ALWAYS SAY

....

....

....

I LOVE YOU MORE THAN

....

....

....

GAME I LIKE TO PLAY
WITH YOU IS

. . . .

. . . .

. . . .

YOU ARE KIND OF PERSON WHO ALWAYS

. . . .

. . . .

. . . .

YOU ARE PROUD OF ME WHEN I

....

....

....

YOU ARE A PERFECT

....

....

....

I WANT YOU TO KNOW
THAT I WILL

. . . .

. . . .

. . . .

I LOVE IT WHEN YOU

....

....

....

Made in the USA
Monee, IL
15 October 2020